The Bear Father Christmas Forgot

By Diana Kimpton
Illustrated by Anna Kiernan

To Madeleine - DK
For my Mum and Dad with love - AK

Scholastic Children's Books,
Commonwealth House, 1-19 New Oxford Street,
London WC1A 1NU, UK
a division of Scholastic Ltd

London ~ New York ~ Toronto ~ Sydney ~ Auckland
Mexico City ~ New Delhi ~ Hong Kong

First published by Scholastic Ltd, 1994
This edition published by Little Hippo, an imprint of Scholastic Ltd, 2000

ISBN 0 439 99715 1

Printed in Belgium

Christmas Eve was nearly over. Father Christmas yawned. Just one more visit to make and then he could go home.

The sleigh landed gently on Madeleine's roof. Father Christmas put the last few toys into a sack and swung it onto his back. But the sack was old. It had a hole in one corner.

"EEEK," said the bear, as he slid through the hole.

"OUCH," said the bear as he landed with a bump on the floor of the sleigh.

He sat up and rubbed his head. He could see Father Christmas climbing down Madeleine's chimney without him. That wasn't right.

He was Madeleine's bear. The label round his neck said so. She had asked Father Christmas for him weeks ago. What would she say in the morning when he wasn't there?

4

For Madeleine

When Father Christmas came back, he didn't
notice the teddy bear sitting all by himself.
He just climbed onto the sleigh and whistled
to his reindeer. They galloped away, pulling
the sleigh up into the night sky.

First the sleigh turned to the right.

"Oops," said the bear, as he tumbled across the floor.

"Ouch," said the bear, as he bumped into the side of the sleigh.

Then the sleigh turned to the left.

"Oops," said the bear, as he tumbled across the floor.

"Ouch," said the bear, as he bumped into the other side of the sleigh.

Next the front of the sleigh pointed up into the air, as the reindeer galloped higher and higher.

"Oops," said the bear, as he tumbled across the floor.

"Help," cried the bear, as he bounced out of the back of the sleigh.

The bear grabbed desperately for something to save
him. As the sleigh flew off, the teddy bear dangled
from the back by his front paws.

"Phew," said the bear, as he held on very tight. His paws ached, but at least he was safe. Then he looked down and saw the roof of Madeleine's house far below him. "That's where I should be," he thought. "If Father Christmas won't take me, I'll have to go by myself." The bear shut his eyes and let go.

"Aaargh," said the bear as he fell through the air.

"Eeek," said the bear as he spun round and round
with his arms and legs outstretched.

"Ouch," said the bear as he landed with a thump on Madeleine's roof.

He sat up and blew some snow off the end of his nose. The snow was cold and damp. It made his fur go spiky.

The bear scrambled up a pile of snow and looked down the chimney.

Inside it was dark and scary. He didn't want to go down there, but how else could he get into Madeleine's house?

"Oooh," said the bear as he climbed nervously into the chimney pot.

"Aargh," cried the bear, as he slid down the chimney.

"Ouch," said the bear, as he landed in the fireplace
with a cloud of soot and ash.

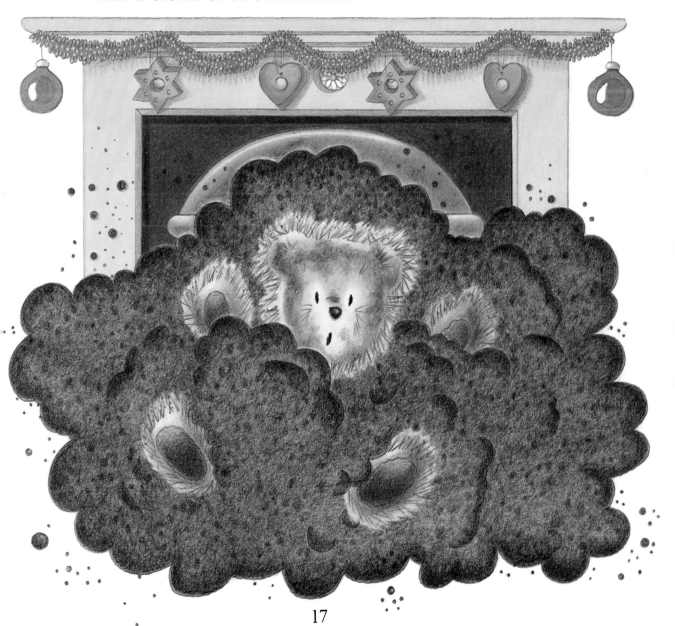

There was no Christmas stocking by the fireplace.
There was no Christmas stocking under the tree.
"It must be beside Madeleine's bed," thought the bear,
so he started to climb the stairs...

The stairs were very tall for a bear. The stairs were very steep for a bear.

"Phew," said the bear when he got to the top.
He wanted to stop for a rest but he couldn't.
He had to hurry. It was nearly morning.

He walked along the landing and peeped around the first door.

"Hmmm," said the bear with a shake of his head. He could hear a dripping tap. He could smell soap.

This wasn't Madeleine's room.

He peeped around the second door.
"Hmmm," said the bear, with a shake of his
head. He could see a big bed with two people
in it. He could hear someone snoring.

This wasn't Madeleine's room.

He peeped around the third door. "Ah-ha," said the
bear. He could see a little girl fast asleep. He could see
a Christmas stocking hanging on the end of her bed.

This must be Madeleine's room.

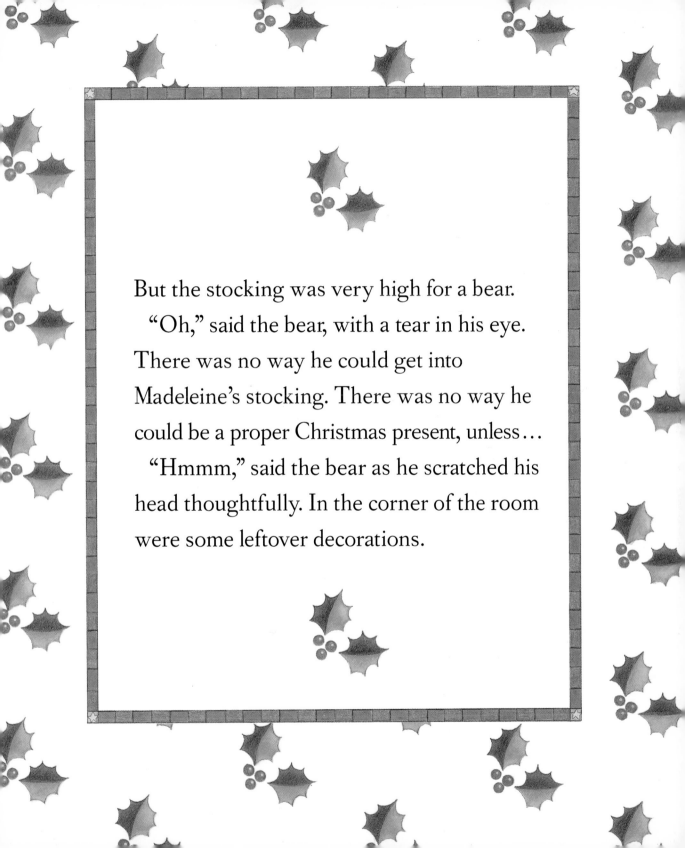

But the stocking was very high for a bear.

"Oh," said the bear, with a tear in his eye. There was no way he could get into Madeleine's stocking. There was no way he could be a proper Christmas present, unless…

"Hmmm," said the bear as he scratched his head thoughtfully. In the corner of the room were some leftover decorations.

"Ho, ho," said the bear, as he rolled himself up in a sheet of wrapping paper.

"Eeek," said the bear, as he fell flat on his back.

"Aaah," said the bear as he looked up at the stocking.

He was badly wrapped up, a little bit damp and rather sooty, but he was in just the right place – well, nearly, anyway.

That's where Madeleine found him in the morning...

and she loved him   straight away.